Please Don't Tell

Jeff Gottesfeld

red rhino books®

Blackout
Body Switch
The Brothers
The Cat Whisperer
Clan Castles
Clan Castles 2: Upgrade Pack
The Code
Fight School
Fish Boy
Flyer
The Forever Boy
The Garden Troll
Ghost Mountain
The Gift
The Hero of Crow's Crossing
Home Planet
I Am Underdog
Killer Flood
Little Miss Miss
The Lost House
The Love Mints
The Magic Stone
One Amazing Summer
Out of Gas
Please Don't Tell
Racer
Sky Watchers
The Soldier
Space Trip
Standing by Emma
Starstruck
Stolen Treasure
Stones
Too Many Dogs
World's Ugliest Dog
Zombies!
Zuze and the Star

ISBN-13: 978-1-62250-964-5
ISBN-10: 1-62250-964-1
eBook: 978-1-63078-479-9

Printed in Malaysia

21 20 19 18 17   1 2 3 4 5

Piper

Age: 12

Allergic To: paper

Hobby: collecting marbles

Favorite Sport: volleyball

Best Quality: honesty

CHARACTERS

Sandy

Age: 12

Favorite Emoji: smiley face with tears of joy

Hidden Talent: clog dancing

Big Secret: still watches cartoons

Best Quality: confidence

1

THE STRANGER

Piper Lewis looked around the room. It was just like last year. And the year before that. All the same kids were there. They wanted a part in the school play.

Piper knew all the faces. There was her best friend, May Park. Ava Woods was cute

but mean. Mark Fisher was nice but geeky. There were a few others too.

About ten kids liked plays. They always tried out. Mr. Green wrote the plays. The teacher liked the theater. He taught sixth grade.

"This place never changes," Piper said to May.

May smiled. She shook out her hair. It was long and dark. May liked to have fun. She didn't care much about grades. But her dad did.

Piper loved school. She loved to learn. Knowing fun facts was her specialty.

Piper and May met when they were little. Their parents were friends first. They moved to the town at the same time. Then the girls became friends. They were close, like sisters. They did everything together. The two liked the same things.

One thing they did not like? A girl in their class. Ava Woods. Ava was mean. Not just mean. She was *evil*. But she was good at acting. Ava always got the best part.

"What is the play about?" May asked.

The door opened. Piper turned to look. It was Mr. Green. He came into the room. "We're about to find out," Piper said.

Mr. Green called to the kids. "Line up! It's time to try out."

The kids lined up. Mr. Green gave them scripts. "My play is about a rabbit. It wants to be a fox. The play is called *The Rabbit and the Fox*."

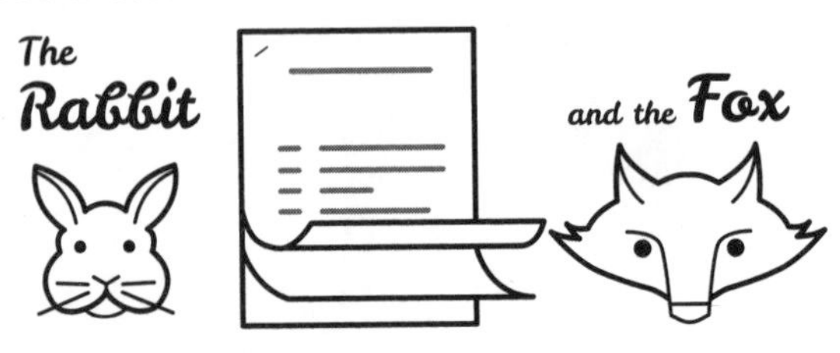

"Clever," May joked.

"Are there any songs?" Ava asked.

"No," Mr. Green said. "But there is a sword fight."

"I want to sing," Ava said.

“I’ll add a song. But only if you get the lead,” Mr. Green said.

Ava laughed. “You better write it now. What is the main part? Bugs Bunny?”

Mr. Green sighed. “The name is not Bugs. It’s Twitch. But yes. The rabbit is the main part.”

“Well, I’m getting it,” Ava said.

“Turn to page nine,” Mr. Green said.

Piper looked at the lines. The story was simple. The fox wanted to eat the rabbit.

The rabbit tried to scare the fox. The hunter wanted to catch the fox. It was a comedy.

"Piper and Mark. You're first," Mr. Green said.

Piper was the rabbit. Mark was the fox.

Piper: You don't look foxy.

Mark: And you don't look like lunch. You look like dinner.

Piper: You can't eat me. I'm sick. I have rabbit fever. One bite and down you go.

Mark: Only one thing is going down. That's you. Down into my belly. Run, rabbit!

The scene was over. The kids clapped.

Piper went back to sit with May. "How did I do?"

"Okay," May said. "But Ava will get the part. Mr. Green loves her."

Ava did get the main part. Piper got a part too. She was the fox. May was the hunter.

"This is not Broadway," Piper joked.

Piper and May left the school. They saw a car pull up. A girl got out.

"Redhead alert," May called out.

"She has great hair," Piper said. She thought the girl was pretty. Even prettier than Ava. "I wonder if she's new." Maybe this girl could act. Ava might have to compete. That would be a first.

Two adults got out of the car. They walked the girl into the school.

2
REDHEAD IN THE ROOM

It was the next day. Piper and May got to class. The redheaded girl was there. She was talking to Mr. Green. It was true. She was new to the school.

The bell rang. "Quiet!" Mr. Green called out. The new girl stood next to him. She

wore jeans and a white blouse. Her hair was tied back.

Piper felt like she knew this girl. But from where? Then she thought of it. The girl looked like a kid actress from the movies. Was this Sandra Melton? No. It couldn't be. This girl had red hair. And why would a big star be here?

"This is Sandy Smith," the teacher said. "She's joining our class. Please welcome her." Some kids clapped. "Now let's get out our math."

Sandy walked to a seat in the back. Piper saw the boys whispering. They were happy about the new girl. She was cute.

Ava frowned. She had been the cutest girl.

Piper was excited. She wanted to talk to the new girl. Tell her about the town. Maybe show her around. There wasn't much to see. But there was the diner. Piper's mom and dad ran it. Maybe Sandy could come in sometime.

It was the middle of the morning. Time for a break. The kids got thirty minutes outside. A dodge ball game started. Piper went up to Sandy.

"Hi! I'm Piper. I'm glad you're here."

"Hi. I'm Sandy."

Three words. Well, it was a start.

"Hi, Sandy. Want to play dodge ball?"

"No thanks. I don't like that game."

Huh? Most kids loved dodge ball. Oh, maybe playing made Sandy too hot. It was all that red hair. It made her sweat. That had to be it.

"I get it," Piper said. "Some kids go to the lunchroom. They play cards. Or they play games on their phones. I can take you there."

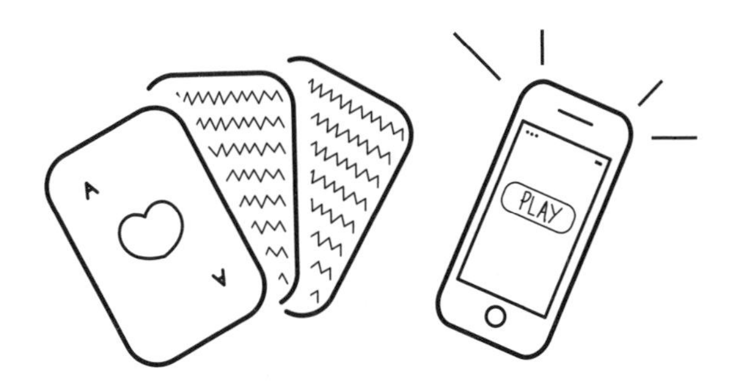

Sandy shook her head. "No thanks."

She doesn't like any games, Piper thought. *Then what?*

"What do you like to do?"

"Read."

A ball rolled over to them. Piper kicked it back to the kids playing. "Our library is small. But you can read there."

"It's okay. I read on my phone. I'm going now. Bye." Sandy turned to go.

"Hey, Sandy?"

Sandy stopped and looked back.

"My parents own a diner. It's on Main Street. Come in sometime. I'll give you a smoothie."

"Maybe." Then she walked away.

May came up to Piper. "What's she like?"

"She doesn't talk much."

"Oh well, you tried. Let's play ball."

May joined the game. Piper looked back at the school. Sandy was going inside. She was a quiet girl. Or maybe she just wasn't friendly.

3
THE SEARCH

All day kids went up to Sandy. They tried to talk to her. Girls. Boys. Even Ava. It was the same each time. The new girl had nothing to say. She wanted to be left alone.

"She's stuck-up," Ava had said. "No one should talk to her. Let her see how it feels. And she's not *that* pretty."

Piper wasn't sure about Sandy. Maybe she wasn't stuck-up. She could just be shy. Or she needed to hide something.

There was one way to find out. She could go online. Search the new girl's name. She had never looked up a kid before.

Piper told May her plan after school. They walked to Piper's house.

The girls were in Piper's room. "You sure you want to do this?" May asked.

Piper shook her head. "No. Am I bad?" She opened her laptop.

"No. Do it."

Piper typed into the search box. *Sandy Smith*. A long list came up. "Oh no!" There were so many hits.

"Try Sandra Smith," May said.

Piper tried it. Not as many. But still too many. It was a good try. But it ended up a total fail.

4

THE DINER

It was the weekend. Piper had to work. The diner was busy. She had not seen the front door open. But now she looked over. Three people stood there. It was Sandy. Two adults were with her. A man and a woman. The woman wore sunglasses.

Piper went over to them. "Hello! Please come with me." She led them to a table.

The adults sat on one side. Sandy sat across from them. Piper gave them menus. Then she went over to her mom.

"See that girl? The one with the red hair? She's new at my school. I think those are her parents. Can I wait on them?"

"Sure," her mom said.

Piper walked up to the table. "Hi, Sandy," she said. Then she looked at the adults. Sandy's mom still had her sunglasses on. Maybe the light hurt her eyes. Or she was famous. That would be funny. No one famous ever came to this town.

"I'm Piper Lewis. I go to school with Sandy. This is my parents' diner." Then she asked for their orders.

Sandy's mom ordered broth. Her dad wanted a veggie burger. It was not on the menu. He asked that it be gluten-free. Piper said she would ask the cook. The man also wanted green tea. Sandy asked for a salad. "*No* dressing," her mom said.

Piper took the order to the kitchen. Everything had to be perfect. And it was. The service was quick. The food was fresh. Even the burger was made just right.

The family was done eating. Piper went over to them. "How was your meal?"

"It was … fine," Sandy's dad said.

"Would you like anything else?"

"Just the check," Sandy's mom said. "We need to go."

"Sure," Piper said. She looked at the table. Sandy's dad had not eaten all of his burger. "Can I bring you a box?" Piper asked.

Sandy's mom stood up. She headed toward the door.

"No," Sandy's dad said.

“Okay,” Piper said. “I’ll get the check.”

She came right back. The check was in her hand. Sandy’s dad took it. He looked at it. Then he placed a few bills on the table.

Piper knew it was too much money. *They must be rich*, she thought.

“Keep the change,” he said. “Come on, Sandy.” He stood up. Then he walked away.

“Thank you,” Piper said. “Come back soon.”

Sandy stood. She put something into Piper’s hand. Then she left the diner.

Piper’s mom walked up. “How did it go?”

"I'm not sure," Piper said.

"Well, you were a good host." Someone called her from across the room. She walked away.

Piper read the note.

Hi Piper.
Sorry I didn't talk much. My parents don't want me to meet new kids. But I need a friend. Can you text me?
Please don't tell.
Sandy

my numbe

Her phone number was there too. Whoa! Sandy was not stuck-up. She was scared.

5
FLYING

It was the next day. Piper told May about the note. They decided to text Sandy. "Can you hang out?"

Sandy texted right back. Her parents wouldn't like it. But they were gone for the day. She wanted to hang out.

"Do you have a bike?" Piper texted.

"Yes."

"Meet me and May at the diner."

The three girls met at the diner. Piper wore a big backpack. She had a plan. They rode their bikes through town. They were headed for the park.

"I don't bike a lot. I'm already tired," Sandy said. "Is it far?"

"Not at all," Piper said. "It's like four more minutes, tops."

They soon got to the park. It was a great spot. There were just a few trees. And there was plenty of room to run. The wind was steady. It wasn't too strong.

Piper stopped under a tree. The girls parked their bikes.

"What do we do now?" Sandy asked.

"Have fun," Piper said. She opened her backpack. "I have kite kits." She took out the kits and string. "We put the kites together. Then we fly."

"I never flew a kite. Will I mess it up? I don't want to," Sandy said. "What if mine

lands in a tree? Or crashes? I'm not good at stuff like this."

"Try it and see," May said. "It's fun."

The girls put their kites together. Piper's was black. May's was green. Sandy's was red like her hair.

The wind was perfect. The kites went right up. Sandy got her kite high in the air. It looked like a dot in the sky. Then the girls had kite wars. Sandy flew her kite into May's. It came down and crashed.

"Yay!" Sandy cried. "I'm a kite killer!"

The girls cracked up. They fixed May's

kite with tape. Then there were more wars. After a while they took a break. Piper had bottled water for everyone. They sat and talked.

Sandy did not say much. But Piper found out two things. The girl loved music. And she liked to cook. "I'm a good cook," she said.

May touched one of Sandy's red locks. "You're so lucky," she told her. "I wish I had hair like yours."

"Thanks, Mom. Thanks, Dad," Sandy said.

Piper frowned. "Your parents don't have red hair."

Sandy nodded. "True. It changed as they got older. I hope mine lasts."

"It must take forever to dry," Piper said. Then she had an idea. She had the scripts to the school play. She took them out of her backpack.

"Hey," Piper said. "What do you think about plays?"

Sandy seemed surprised. "Plays? What about them? What do you want to know? If I act? Why are you asking?"

Piper thought this was odd. It was no big thing. “Sorry. I didn’t mean to upset you.”

“Piper and I love plays,” May said.

Sandy crossed her fingers. They were in the shape of an *X*. “No plays for me. No acting.”

“It could be like flying the kite,” May said. “You weren’t sure about that. But you tried. And you did it. Maybe it’s the same with acting.”

“I told you. *No* acting,” Sandy said.

“Got it,” Piper said. “May and I are in

the play. It opens in two weeks. Mr. Green wrote it. We need to learn our lines. Can you help us?"

Sandy gulped. "Um ... sure. But I won't be in the play. Just so you know."

Piper gave May a script. She took one for herself. "You and May can share," she told Sandy. "I'm the fox. May is the hunter. You read the rabbit. Okay?"

"Okay," Sandy said. She did not look happy.

They each read their lines. Sandy was super good as the rabbit. Way better than Ava. Sandy was a pro.

The scene ended. Piper pumped her arms. “Sandy? I hate to say it. But you can act.”

The girl shook her head. “No I can’t. I stink.”

May touched Sandy’s arm. “Not true. Piper is all about the truth. She said you’re great. And you are. Too bad Ava is playing the rabbit.”

“Yeah,” Piper said. “The other parts are taken too.”

“Someone might get sick. Or have to drop out,” May said. “Then Sandy can step in.”

“Yeah,” Piper said. “Mark dropped out last year. Remember? He got the flu.”

May nodded. “We need to tell Mr. Green.”

Sandy stood up. She looked down at the girls. Her eyes blazed. “I’ll say this one more time. I won’t be in your play. There’s no way. So don’t bring it up again. Please!”

6

SANDY SPEAKS

The girls rode back to town. No one said a word. Not about the play. Or anything else. Soon they were at the diner. They locked their bikes. Then they went inside.

Piper found a table. May and Sandy sat down. Then Piper went to the kitchen. A minute later she was back. She set a tray

on the table. "I have juice and muffins," she said. Then Piper sat down. She looked over at May and Sandy.

"It must be fun to work here," Sandy said. "I bet you eat a lot. Do you worry about getting fat?"

"Not really," Piper said. "We make healthy foods. And I bike a lot. I walk a lot too."

Sandy laughed. "The girls where I'm from are afraid of fat. They make a big deal about food. They're like, 'Oh! I'm so fat! I'm the size of a car! I can't eat one more thing.

That's it. I'm sewing my lips shut. I won't ever eat again. Then I can be cute.' "

Piper and May laughed.

"You are so good at acting," May said.

"That's not acting. That's just me," Sandy said. She picked up a muffin. "I love to eat." She took a big bite.

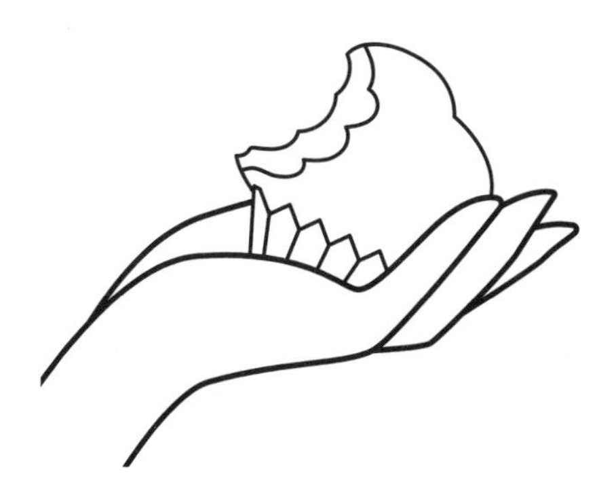

May was still laughing. But Piper was thinking. Sandy had said something. "*Where I'm from.*" Maybe she would open up.

"So," Piper said. "Where did you live before? Before you came here?"

"I don't have a real home. I move around with my folks. They work for the government. We go away for two years. Then we come back. We pick a new home every time. France. China. All over. This is our first small town."

"But you talked about those girls," Piper said. "They sounded like good friends. Where was that?"

"I met those girls in Paris."

"Do you speak French?" May asked.

Sandy said a few words.

"I guess you do," Piper said. "Do you make French food? We can do a dinner."

"I'm not a very good cook," Sandy said.

May stopped her. "That's not what you said before."

Sandy's face was red. "Well … I can cook. But there is good. And there is very good. They're not the same."

"I guess," Piper said. She didn't know what to say. Maybe she would take a picture. It seemed like a good time.

Piper got up. She went over to her friends. She leaned down between them. Then she held up her phone.

"Smile," Piper said.

Sandy leaned to one side. "No pictures!"

Piper put her phone down. She looked at Sandy. First the girl got mad about acting. Now this. What was her problem? "Sorry. I thought it would be fun."

Sandy changed the subject. "Tell me about the diner. How long have you guys had it?"

Piper told the story. Her family moved here seven years ago. They bought the diner. Business was good. But Piper's mind was on something else. Sandy's stories about Paris and cooking. They didn't sound right.

And what about the picture? Why did she get upset? Piper was pretty sure of one thing. Sandy was lying.

7
SANDY'S CHANCE

It was before school on Monday. Sandy came up to the girls.

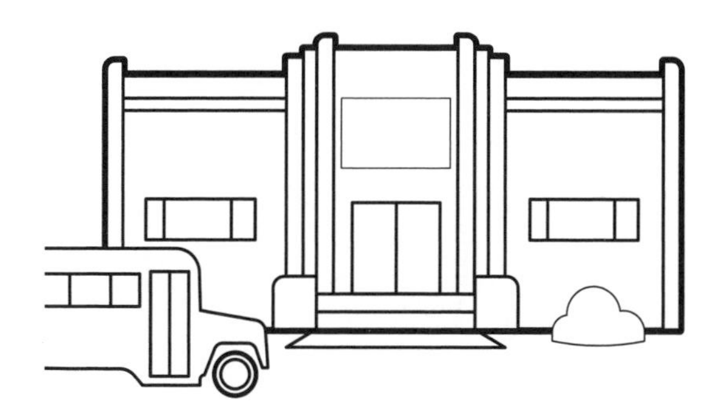

"I had fun with you guys," she said.

Really? Piper thought. Then she smiled. "We did too."

"Look," Sandy said. "I need your help. It's like I told you. My parents are kind of nuts.

They don't want me around kids. They say it's not good for me. I don't agree. But I don't want to make them mad. So here's the deal. Don't say hello if I'm with them. I may be cold to other kids. Just know I don't mean it. Are we cool?"

Piper nodded. "It's all good." But it seemed crazy. She was glad she wasn't Sandy.

"I'm in too," May said.

"Great," Sandy said. Then she hugged them. First May, then Piper.

Sandy was a little shorter than Piper.

Piper could see the top of the girl's head. Wow! Something had changed. She was sure of it.

Just then five kids burst into the room. They all talked at once.

"Did you hear? Ava broke her arm!"

"In two places."

"Mark said she was hit by a car!"

"Cool it, you guys. I just saw her outside. She's coming."

Ava came into the room. Her right arm was in a cast. It went up above her elbow.

Kids wanted to sign it. Ava shooed them away.

"I tripped over my cat," she said. "You know what this means? I can't be in the play. There's a sword fight. But I can't fence. I have to drop out. So don't ask to sign my cast. I hate it!"

Mr. Green came into the room. He saw Ava in the cast. "Ava! What happened?"

Ava told him. Mr. Green sighed. He had lost his star. The teacher turned to the class. "Well, someone tell me. Who can act? Speak up now."

Piper and May looked at Sandy. Sandy shook her head. "I can't. Get it? *I can't.*"

No way! Piper did not get it. They needed Sandy. Why wouldn't she help?

8

NO TRACE

Piper had an idea. May's dad worked at the post office. There were records of everyone. He could look up Sandy's name. Maybe find her old address.

The girls went to May's house after school.

"What do you think of Sandy's hair?" Piper asked.

"I would kill for it," May joked.

"Sad news. It's not hers."

"What? It's a wig?"

"Nope. I saw the top of her head. She's got roots. Dark ones."

May bit her lower lip. "Wow! She said the color was real."

May's dad came in the front door. "Hey, sweet May. Hey, Piper. Are you here to do homework?"

"Soon," May said. "Can you do us a favor, Dad?"

Mr. Park stood in the front hall. “Maybe. What’s up?”

“There’s this new girl at school,” Piper said. “No one knows where she’s from.”

“What does she say?”

“She’s not from anywhere. She’s lived in a lot of places. In other countries too,” May said.

“It could be true,” Mr. Park said.

“Can you check her last address?” May asked.

“Hold on now. That sounds like spying. What’s going on? Why are you so curious about this girl?”

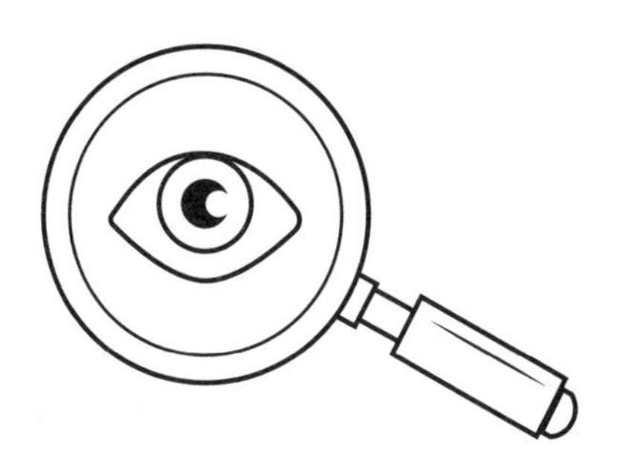

"She's not like any kids we know," May said.

"It's like she has a secret," Piper said. "We want to figure it out."

"I'll look up the current address," Mr. Park said. "But that's it." He went over to his laptop. The girls stood next to him.

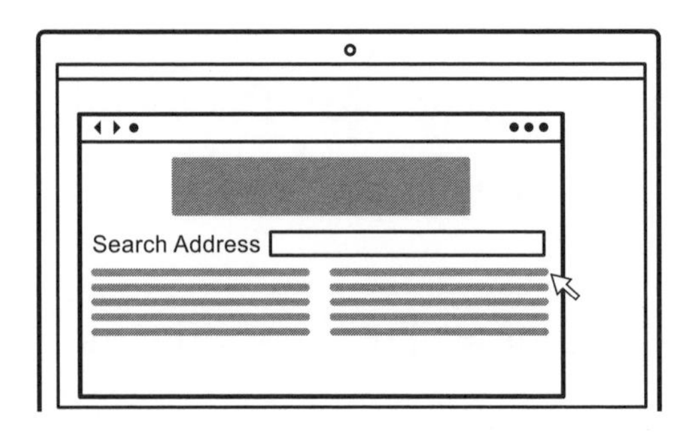

He pulled up a website. It listed all the streets in town. He quickly found Sandy's house. "Mr. Barry Smith and Mrs. Mary Smith. You know, girls. Some people *do* move around a lot. It could be for work. Or they get tired of a place. Okay," Mr. Park

said. "I'm going to change. Walk the dog, May. Then do your homework."

May's dad had left the room. Piper folded her arms. "No main address. Hair color not real. Does not want friends. Can act but won't be in the play. Will not have her picture taken. What does all that say?"

May shrugged.

"I know. Sandy and her parents *do* have a secret. They don't want people to know where they are. But why?"

9

THE TRUTH

May was ready to walk the dog. Piper said she'd go too. They left the house. The girls had little to say.

"Thinking about Sandy?" May asked. Max walked next to her.

"What else? I like Sandy as a friend.

Dropping her would suck. But this has to stop. Friends should not keep secrets."

Max stopped to sniff a tree. May waited. "What will you do?"

"Talk to her. Tell her what we think. And tell her things have to change."

May nodded. "I'm down with that. When?"

"We know where she lives. Let's go today.

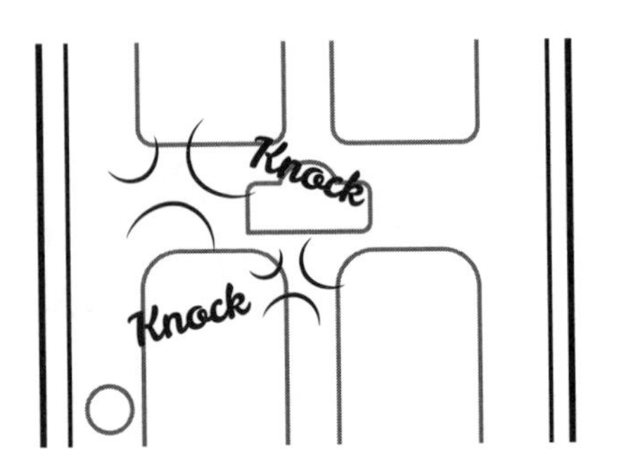

It was an hour later. The dog walk was done. Max was back at home.

Now the girls were at the Smiths'. They stood at the front door. Piper knocked. No one came.

"Try again," May said.

Piper did. Harder this time. The door swung open. Sandy's dad stood there. He was on the phone.

"Yes. She will be there. She'll need some things in her trailer. Cold-pressed juice. Raw nuts. A box of ..." He looked at Piper and May. "I'll call you back." He hung up.

"Hi, Mr. Smith," Piper said. "I met you at the diner. This is May. We're Sandy's friends."

"She has no friends. You need to leave."

Piper took a chance. She called into the house. “Sandy! It’s Piper and May. We need to talk to you and your parents. Please?”

Mr. Smith looked mad. “I told you kids to—”

“It’s okay, Uncle Barry!”

Sandy came to the door. Piper was stunned. Sandy called the man her uncle. He was not her dad.

Just then there was the sound of a car. The girls turned to look. The car pulled up and parked. A woman got out. It was Sandy’s mom. Or maybe her aunt.

She was wearing yoga clothes. And she had on the same sunglasses. A gym bag was over her shoulder. Inside the bag was a tiny dog. Its head was poking out from the top.

"Hi, Aunt Mary. You're just in time. This is Piper and May. The girls from school I like. We need to talk."

What was going on? Why was Sandy in charge?

"You guys have questions. You want to know about me. Am I right?" Sandy asked.

Piper nodded. "Yep."

"Okay. Come inside. I have a surprise. I think you'll like it."

Sandy's aunt walked past the girls. They followed her inside. Piper's heart was beating hard. She was going to get answers. She hoped so anyway.

10
PLEASE DON'T TELL

There were photos on the tables. Someone had signed them. Posters were stacked on the floor. There was a picture on them. It was the kid star Sandra Melton.

Piper looked at the posters. Then she looked at Sandy. Then at the posters. And then at Sandy one more time. No way! It couldn't be. But it was.

"Oh my God!" Piper shouted. She pointed at Sandy. "You're Sandra Melton! You're a big star!"

Now the little dog was yelping. It began to run in circles. Sandy's aunt smiled. She had taken off her sunglasses. "Princess thinks so," she said.

Sandy grinned. "A big star? I don't know. I've made some movies."

"You're a star for sure. But why are you

here?" Piper asked. "And why the red hair? And the fake name? Are you hiding? Does someone want to kill you?"

Sandy's aunt and uncle laughed.

"No, no. It's all good," Sandy said. "I'm here for work. I'm doing a movie next year. *Little Town Blues*. It's set in a small town. But I've never lived in one. The director sent me here. He wanted me to check it out. I'm here for two more weeks. Then I go back to L.A. We film in a month."

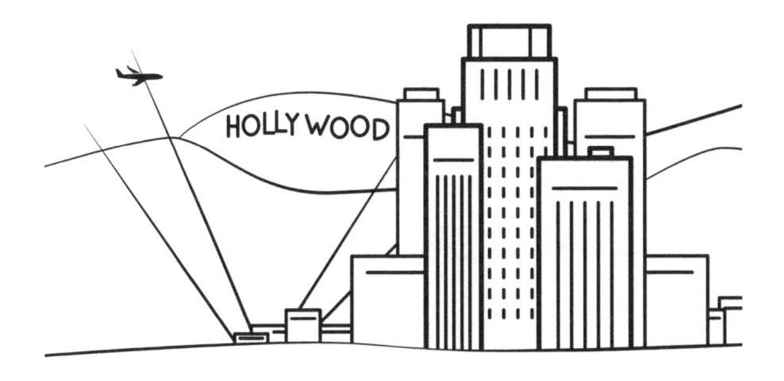

Piper and May jumped up and down. This was not happening!

"Sorry about the lies," Sandy said. "No one is supposed to know I'm me. That's why I told the stories. And changed my hair color. I like it red. Do you?"

Piper knew this was the truth. Sandy was now being herself. She seemed happy.

May jumped in. "But your last name is Smith. That's the name the school has for you."

Sandy giggled. "My acting name is Melton. Smith is my real last name. Uncle Barry is a Smith too. He's my dad's brother.

And he's my agent. I don't always live with my aunt and uncle. Just when I'm doing a movie. Now do you see? This is why I can't be in your play."

Piper and May looked at each other. It was true. Sandy couldn't be in the play. It would be a huge story on the news. "*Big Star in Small-Town School Play!*"

Sandy just wanted to do her job and leave. She had told some lies. But Piper did not blame her.

"I'm sorry if we were rude," Uncle Barry said. "You seem like great girls."

“Now what?” Piper asked Sandy.

“You’ll come to the movie opening. It will be next year,” Sandy said. “Red carpet. The whole thing. Just do one thing for me. Let me do my job. *Please don’t tell.*”

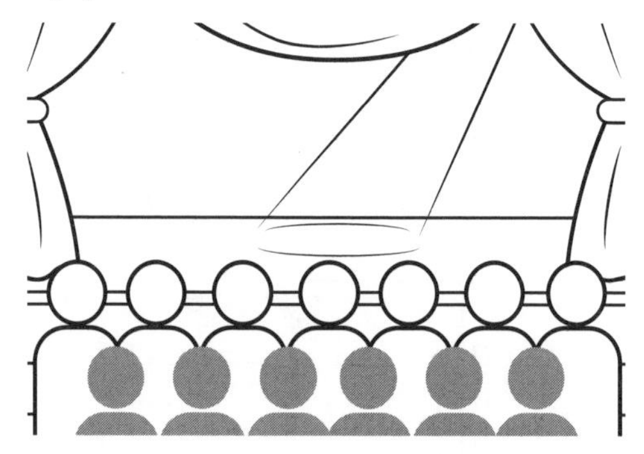

Piper and May kept Sandy’s secret.

Finally it was the night of the play. Piper had the lead role. She was the rabbit. May was now the fox.

The whole town was there. It was a big crowd. Everyone liked the play. They stood and clapped when it ended.

Someone else had seen it all. It was the

new girl with the great hair. This was her last night in town. She brought flowers for the girls. There was a card with them.

To Piper and May.
You guys are great! I go home in the morning. See you in Hollywood. Yes! You can talk about me. But wait till I m gone. Then have fun telling everyone.
Your friend,
Sandy

Piper grinned. Tell everyone? She'd love to. It was a great story.